THE Big Sparkly

Mellow Yellow Unicorn

Competition

WIN!

1ST PRIZE

TERMS & CONDITIONS APPLY.

TO WIN THIS FABULOUS
UNICORN...

Easy!

▶ BAKE A RAINBOW CAKE!

▶ MAKE A MAGIC CASTLE!

▶ DESIGN A UNICORN FAIRY COSTUME!

▶ GIVE YOUR BEST PERFORMANCE!

ORCHARD BOOKS
First published in Great Britain in 2018 by
The Watts Publishing Group
1 3 5 7 9 10 8 6 4 2
Text and illustrations © Fabi Santiago 2018
The moral rights of the author have been asserted.
A CIP catalogue record for this book is available from the British Library.
HB ISBN 978 1 40833 690 8 • PB ISBN 978 1 40833 691 5
Printed and bound in China

MIX
Paper from
responsible sources
FSC
www.fsc.org
FSC® C104740

Orchard Books, an imprint of Hachette Children's Group,
part of The Watts Publishing Group Limited
Carmelite House, 50 Victoria Embankment, London EC4Y 0DZ
An Hachette UK Company
www.hachette.co.uk
www.hachettechildrens.co.uk

The Mellow Yellow Unicorn looked very shiny in the toyshop window with its glow-in-the-dark horn. There was only one way to own it, and that was by winning Miss Twinkletoes' talent competition. EVERYONE wanted the unicorn, especially . . .

# ...CHLOE,

who wore a red ribbon

on her head

and was very good at

unicycle stunts.

I REALLY want that unicorn, thought Chloe. All I have to do is . . .

bake a rainbow cake,

make a magic castle,

design a unicorn fairy costume

and give my best performance.

Easy!

There was just one

problem . . .

... **VERONICA**,

who wore a yellow ribbon on her head,
and was VERY good at hula-hooping
(and all sorts of other things).

Veronica also wanted to win the
Mellow Yellow Unicorn.

With only two weeks to go, Chloe got busy . . .

baking a rainbow cake, making a magic castle . . .

sewing a unicorn fairy costume and practising a winning performance.

# So did **Veronica**.

THE BIG SPARKLY MELLOW YELLOW

Eventually the big day arrived. The children gathered round
as Miss Twinkletoes brought out the Mellow Yellow Unicorn.

Chloe's heart leapt. It was beautiful. It was perfect!

"Let the competition begin," said Miss Twinkletoes.

First came the baking round.

Everyone gasped in amazement as Chloe revealed her rainbow unicorn cake.

But then **Veronica** arrived

with a
# MUCH BIGGER,
# MUCH SPARKLIER
rainbow unicorn cake.

Never mind,

thought Chloe.

My magic castle is
**really** good . . .

But Veronica's castle was

# REALLY, REALLY

good . . .

. . . and her

unicorn fairy costume

was perfect.

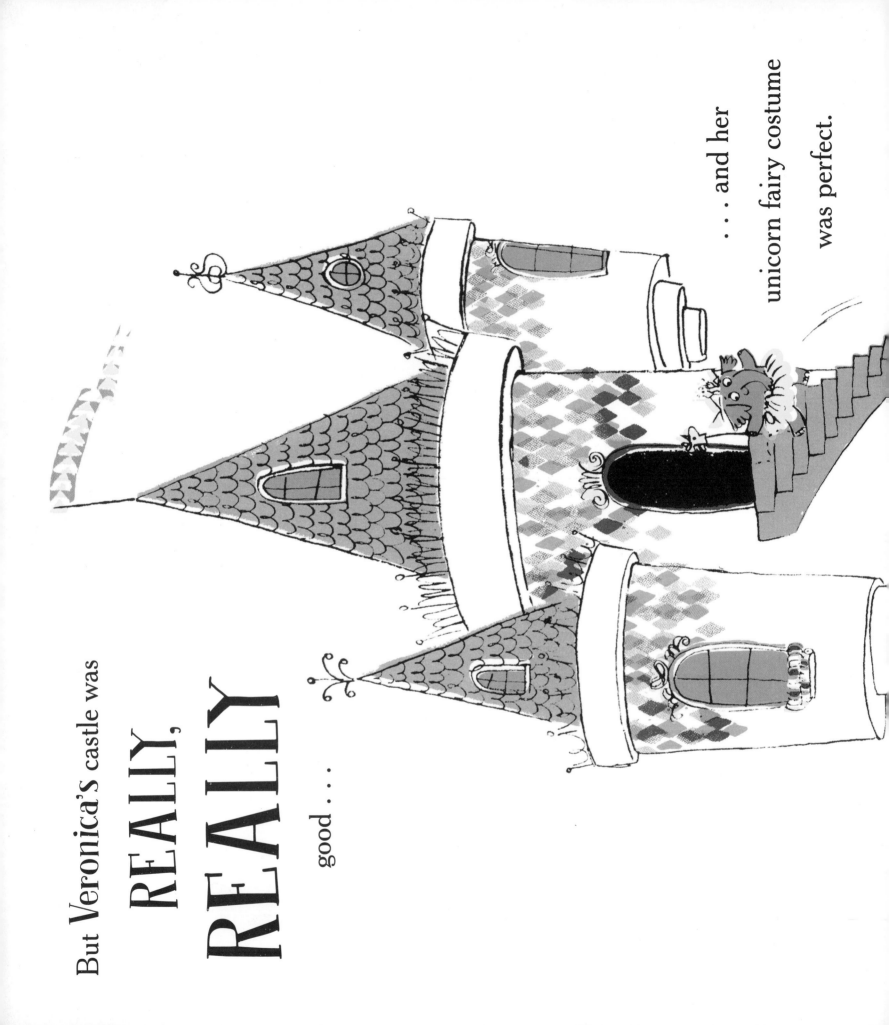

Chloe had
one last chance.

It was time for everyone to

give their performances.

Veronica's hula-hooping was GREAT.

Chloe's unicycling was AMAZING!

But whose performance would

Miss Twinkletoes like best?

The audience was silent as Miss Twinkletoes
made her decision. It took AGES.

Finally she stepped forward.

"And the winner is...

Chloe was flabbergasted.

A flying one-hippo band?

So was **Veronica**.
They hadn't seen **that** coming.

Why didn't
we think of
that?

And **Fabrizio?**

He was . . .

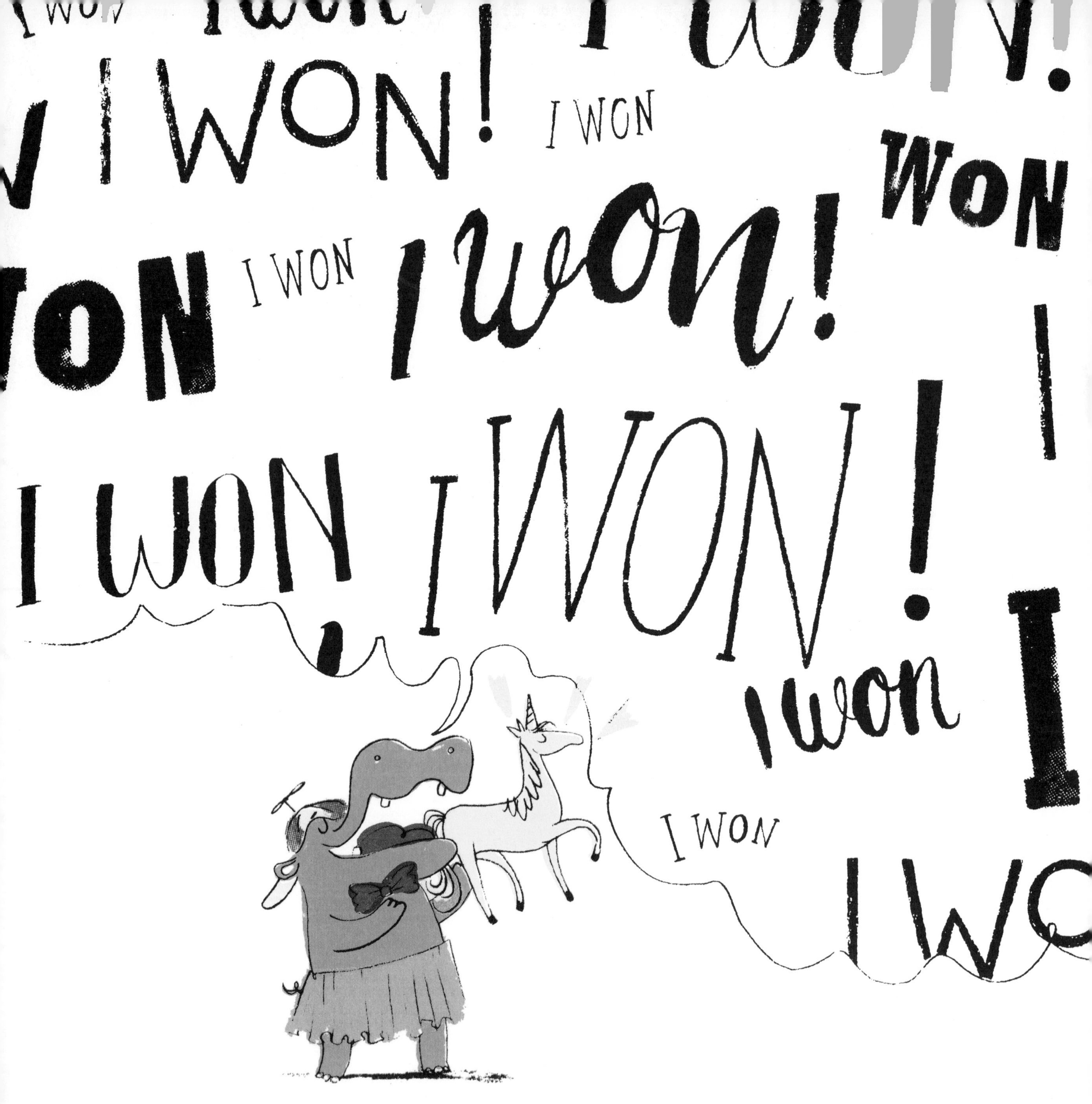
I WON!
I WON
WON
I WON
I won!
I WON
I WON!
I won
I WON

... **VERY, VERY** good at boasting. Chloe and Veronica
agreed about that – and they agreed about something else too ...

The Mellow Yellow Unicorn

was brilliant – but being friends was

MUCH MORE FUN.

Right?